# REKKAR
## THE SCREECHING ORCA

*With special thanks to Michael Ford*

For James and Fiona

www.seaquestbooks.co.uk

ORCHARD BOOKS
338 Euston Road, London NW1 3BH
*Orchard Books Australia*
Level 17/207 Kent St, Sydney, NSW 2000

A Paperback Original
First published in Great Britain in 2014

Sea Quest is a registered trademark of Beast Quest Limited
Series created by Beast Quest Limited, London

A CIP catalogue record for this book is available from
the British Library.

ISBN 978 1 40832 861 3

1 3 5 7 9 10 8 6 4 2

Printed in Great Britain by CPI Group (UK) Ltd, Croydon, CR0 4YY

The paper and board used in this paperback are natural recyclable
products made from wood grown in sustainable forests. The
manufacturing processes conform to the environmental regulations of
the country of origin.

Orchard Books is a division of Hachette Children's Books,
an Hachette UK company

www.hachette.co.uk

# REKKAR
## THE SCREECHING ORCA

## BY ADAM BLADE

ORCHARD

I'm coming for you, Max!

You think you have defeated me -
the mighty Cora Blackheart? Idiot
boy! You've only made me angry!
I may have lost my ship and my
crew, but it's not over. Now it's
just you and me...and the deadly
Robobeasts under my control!

You have something that I want, Max
- an object so powerful, I can use
it to rule all of Nemos! And you
don't even know it...

But first I will destroy your
whole family - your mother, your
father...and that irritating Merryn
girl, too.

Cora Blackheart will have her
revenge!

# CHAPTER ONE

# THE LEAPING DOLPHIN RETURNS

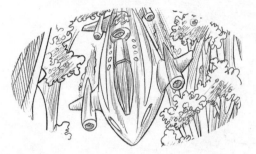

**M**ax crouched on a platform, welding torch in hand, working on the body of the *Leaping Dolphin II*. The submarine was held in place above the water by four huge clamps. As Max directed the blue flame over the join between two metal plates, sparks showered off the hull and sizzled when they hit the water. Meanwhile his dogbot Rivet dashed back and forth, trying to catch the sparks in his mouth.

Beyond the docks, the tall skyscrapers of the city rose like needles into the clouds. Transports hovered through the streets, and cranes lifted huge steel beams into place. Since Cora Blackheart's attack just weeks earlier, the repairs had gone on day and night. Her Robobeast Chakrol had destroyed a huge section of the city's titanium defence shield and left much of the fleet badly damaged.

The waves beside the dock stirred and Max's friend Lia's head emerged. Her Amphibio mask dangled from her neck by a strap, and she placed it over her nose and mouth to allow her to breathe above the water. The Merryn princess pushed her silver hair away from her face with a webbed hand.

"Still tinkering with that lump of metal?" she said.

"Rivet not lump!" said Max's robodog.

Max killed the blowtorch and raised his protective visor. "Not any more. I'm done!" he said, feeling a swell of pride in his chest. He patted Rivet's snout. "She's not talking about you, boy." He stood up and admired his handiwork – a full-size replica of the first *Leaping Dolphin*, gleaming in the early morning light – *Leaping Dolphin II. Not just any lump of metal,* thought Max. The submarine's sleek body was shaped like a bullet, with a plexiglass viewing screen at the front and portholes along the side. Four thrusters were positioned at the front and rear, their steel propellers polished to a shine. There was a hatch on top and an airlock for leaving or entering underwater. Emblazoned across the vessel's flank in scarlet paint was a stencil of an arcing dolphin.

Max's mother, Niobe, stuck her head through the hatch. "I'm finished in here too," she said, climbing out and jumping down from the top of the sub. "Hi, Lia!" She stood back and squeezed Max's shoulder. "It looks even better than the original, Max. Thank you!"

Max grinned. The first *Leaping Dolphin* was now a shipwreck, lost beneath the waves. So for the last fortnight, he and his mother had been sourcing parts to build the replacement submarine. Finally, it was ready.

"Shall we take it for a spin?" asked his mother with a wink.

"Now?" said Max, glancing up at the towering skyscraper beside them. Their apartment was on the 523rd floor. "What about Dad?"

"Callum needs his sleep," said his mother. "He's working long shifts on the city's repairs. We'll be back before he's finished breakfast."

"All right then," said Max, excitement bubbling in his stomach. He missed the seas of Nemos. Especially since his aquabike had gone missing from the docks a couple of weeks ago. Someone must have stolen it, and so far the Aquoran cops hadn't managed to track the thief. *They've got plenty of other things to worry about, what with the damaged city*, Max thought glumly.

"I don't get it," said Lia. "It's still just a lump of metal, if you ask me."

The Merryn girl tried to look unimpressed, but Max could tell from the gleam in her eyes she was faking.

"Come on," he said. "Let's take a look inside."

They climbed aboard, dropping through the top hatch. Rivet scrambled through last, dangling for a moment by his front claws before landing with a clang. Much of the interior looked the same as Max remembered – the twin seats at the front covered with red leather, the storage facilities and scanning equipment. But looking closer, Max realised his mother had equipped the new *Leaping Dolphin* with several upgrades. "Awesome!" he said, running his fingers over the controls. The sensors had a longer reach. He switched on the navigation systems and saw they were

Compass 3.0, the most advanced available. "How did you get your hands on this?" he asked.

His mum's eyes shone with excitement. "I pulled a few strings. Check this out." She pushed a button and two gauntlets rose out of the control panel. "Manual grapplers," she

said. "Put your hands in."

Max did as she said, and slid his hands into the gloves. As he did so, two metal claws extended from beneath the sub's nose. They clenched and opened as Max flexed his fingers.

"Cool!" he said. "And what about these?"

He pointed to a bank of switches and a control stick. His mother grabbed his hand and pulled it back. "Those are the new weapons systems," she said gravely. "I've fitted blasters and torpedoes."

Max nodded, feeling suddenly serious. The original *Dolphin* had been an exploratory vessel, but this one could defend itself. *I just hope it doesn't have to.*

"Now, let me show you how fast it can go," said his mother.

Max knew Lia was curious, because instead of getting out, she closed the hatch. He couldn't help smiling as he pressed a button to lower the sub into the sea. The *Dolphin* juddered as it descended, then hit the surface with a light thump.

As the water rose up over the front shield, his limbs tingled with anticipation. Then the waves swamped over the sub and they were fully submerged. The open ocean waited. Niobe slipped into the captain's seat with a creak of leather, and pushed the throttle. With a low hum, the engines kicked in and they shot through the water.

"Wow!" said Max, as the force pushed him back into the co-pilot's chair. Lia grabbed the back of the chair to stop herself from falling over.

"Sorry about that," said Niobe. "These new engines are more powerful than the old ones."

She set the sub to "cruise" and they left

Aquora far behind. The engines gave out a gentle thrum, and the only sounds inside were the soft bleeps of the scanners, mapping the waters and seabed beyond.

A silver shape appeared at the front of the ship, keeping pace.

"Spike!" barked Rivet from Max's side.

Lia's pet swordfish cut through the water with powerful thrusts of his tail. The Merryn girl put her hand to the glass, then frowned. "That's odd," she said. "I'm trying to communicate with my Aqua Powers, but he isn't getting the message." She gestured with a webbed hand at all the flashing lights on the *Dolphin*'s control panels. "Must be all these tech signals messing things up."

"Try outside the sub," said Niobe. "The airlock's at the rear, beside the sleeping quarters."

"Wait a moment," said Max. He went to

a storage panel and took out a small device the size of a matchbox, with a trailing wire shaped into a hook. "I made this for you," he said. "Hold still."

"What is it?" asked Lia.

"It's a brain-fryer," said Max, grinning.

Lia flinched away. "I'm not wearing that!"

Max rolled his eyes. "I'm only joking! It's to let you communicate with us in the sub," he said.

"Oh. Well, in that case…" Lia stayed put while he hooked the device over her ear. The small box sat on her jaw and an earbud slotted into her ear.

The airlock door slid shut behind Lia, and soon she was riding beside them on Spike's back.

Max flicked the switch. "Max to Lia. Testing. Can you hear me? Over," he said.

"I feel stupid wearing this thing," said Lia.

Max laughed. "You'll get used to it."

Niobe was leaning over the controls. Suddenly the sub lurched in the water as it sped off on a new course. Spike fell back for a moment then caught up. Max noticed a mischievous smile on his mother's face.

"Where are we going?" he asked.

His mother tapped a few buttons and a 3D holomap sprang from the control panels. A flashing green line showed their course towards a string of tiny islands. "There," said Niobe, pointing to the largest of the landmasses. "Home."

Max shrugged. "I don't get it – Aquora is home."

"Aquora is my home now, but I lived on that island for a good long while," she said, "hiding from your uncle."

Max leaned forward, eager to hear more. What with Cora's attack and the repairs, he'd barely had a chance to talk to his mother about her "missing years" – the decade she was away from Aquora. He guessed she must have hundreds of stories.

"I set up a lab there," she said, "creating robots to look after the day-to-day stuff while I concentrated on my research, trying to find a way to defeat my brother, or to make him see sense. It was all going well until Cora showed up."

*Cora Blackheart.* Max felt his blood grow hot. The pirate had teamed up with Max's wicked uncle, the Professor, and almost wiped out Aquora with their Robobeasts. Though the Professor was locked up in Aquora's jail, Cora had escaped. *And something tells me she won't lie low for long*, Max thought.

"My brother led Cora to the island," said Niobe. "They kidnapped me. But they left most of my equipment and research records behind – I want to see what we can salvage."

The speakers crackled. "Lia to Breathers. Are you there?"

"Yes?" said Max.

Lia and Spike darted in front of the viewing screen and pointed ahead. "Will your clever tech get you through that?" she asked.

The scanners showed a huge mass ahead, and Max zoomed in on the display. He gasped in wonder. It was an enormous coral reef, its intricate white branches blocking their path.

"Already!" said Niobe. "This sub's even faster than the first *Leaping Dolphin*. We should navigate around the reef, Max. The waters are clear if we approach from the other side."

But Max felt a twinge of pride. *I'm not backing away from a challenge like that!* "Let's show Lia," he said. "I'll take the controls."

"If you're sure," said Max's mum. "But

don't scratch my brand-new paintwork!"

Lia shot off ahead, descending into the coral forest. Max took the controls, switched the sub to manual, and went after her. He tipped the sub sideways to slip between two huge branches of coral like giant bones. Lia

was a silver flash in the distance already, so Max gunned the throttle pedal for more speed.

"You're quite a pilot," said his mother.

Max blushed and lifted the sub's nose over another looming branch of coral.

Niobe pushed the communications button.

"Just be careful out there, Lia," she said. "I set up some defences – they might still be operational."

"I think I can handle a bit of tech!" said Lia's voice.

Max's mum grinned and looked at Max. "I like her. She's feisty. A bit like me at that age."

"Just as stubborn too," teased Max.

"Don't be cheeky," said his mum.

Their laughter was interrupted by a burst of static through the speakers. Max's hands tightened over the controls. "Lia?" he said.

No answer.

The speakers crackled suddenly, and Lia's voice came through loud and clear...and terrified.

"Help!" she cried. "Help me!"

# CHAPTER TWO

# TANGLED!

Max's heart jumped in his chest. He pressed the throttle pedal harder and zipped through the water, jerking the sub from side to side to avoid the coral.

"Slow down!" said his mother. "You'll get us killed if you're not careful."

Max didn't care. Lia's shouts still sounded through the speakers, muffled and panicked.

Then Max saw her. She was struggling in the water, writhing. Spike swam nearby, sawing at the empty water.

*What's going on?*

He hit the reverse thrusters and let the sub drift closer. At ten paces he saw that Spike was actually attacking a super-thin fibre net with his sword-shaped bill. And Lia was trapped inside it! "What in all Nemos..." muttered Max. He'd never seen anything like it. As Lia turned and twisted her body, the net only wrapped more tightly around her.

"Don't move!" said Niobe. "It's steel micro-cord. I designed it myself."

Lia went still in the water, but her face was painted with terror. Max could see the metal biting into her skin.

Quickly he put on another communicator headset, then ran to the back of the sub and opened the airlock, drawing his hyperblade.

"You shouldn't go out there," said Niobe. "We can use the grapplers. I don't know what other defences might still be working."

"I can't leave her like that," Max insisted. He swam out into the sea, letting the water envelop him and breathing through his gills, and kicked towards Lia as fast as he could.

Before he even reached her side, she suddenly rose through the water, winched towards the surface. Max realised with horror that her hands were tied behind her.

*She won't be able to use her Amphibio mask!*

His mother was peering through the viewing screen. "How can we stop it?" Max shouted over the communicator.

"We can't!" came her voice in his ear. "It's automated, controlled from the island."

Max stared, horrified, as Lia was hauled above the water.

Spike watched her too, thrashing in despair. "Fine," said Max. "Then bring a blaster!"

Seconds later, Niobe was swimming from the *Dolphin*'s hatch, clutching her pistol. They surfaced together. Max saw they were near the island now – a short distance away, a barren sandy beach with a few palm trees and clumps of grass rose above the water. Reaching up from the shallows was a huge robotic crane, lifting Lia high above the waves. She was still struggling, but Max could see her gills opening and closing rapidly. She didn't have long.

Max took the blaster from his mum and aimed at the cord stretching from the end of the crane's arm. His first shot went wide. He steadied his hands and fired again. Sparks exploded from the crane, but the cord held.

"INTRUDER! INTRUDER!" cried a shrill electronic voice.

"Orion!" said Max's mother.

Max glanced down and saw two robots skimming across towards them. They looked like metal crabs, each with two pincers and eyes on stalks. *They must be the robots Mum mentioned*, he thought, focusing his attention on Lia, who was suffocating by the second. He took aim again, and pulled the trigger.

Suddenly the blaster was torn from his grip and the shot missed completely. One of the robots had grabbed it, and was skimming back towards the island.

"No!" he screamed.

His mother swam after the bot. "Orion, come back!" she shouted.

Spike leaped high out of the water, trying to reach Lia, but flopped down into the waves uselessly. Max's Merryn friend was moving weakly now, her eyes half closed...

Suddenly, Max had an idea. "Rivet, come here!" he said. The dogbot swam quickly to him. Max gripped his collar. "Dive!" he said.

"Yes, Max!" barked Rivet, and he nosed down under the waves. When he was ten metres down, Max steered him to point upwards. "We need maximum thrust, Riv," he said. "We need to get some height, understand?"

"Big thrust!" barked Rivet.

His boosters fired, and Max held on tight as they shot upwards. "Faster!" he shouted.

Rivet tucked in his legs and angled his nose upwards. They broke free of the water's grip and surged into the sky, straight towards Lia.

Max let go, drawing his hyperblade at the same time. *Here goes…* With a quick cut, he severed the cord just above Lia's head. He would have punched the air in triumph, but there was no time. They both fell, along with Rivet, back into the water below.

Through a cloud of bubbles Max searched for Lia. She was floating underwater, hardly moving, and still tangled in the net. But her eyelids were fluttering. She was alive.

Spike was already pressing close to her side, and Max found the edge of the mesh and carefully untangled it, tugging her loose. By the time he'd finished, her eyes were open.

"I really *hate* technology," she said.

Max smiled, but his pulse was still racing. "For once, I agree with you," he said.

Lia stroked the swordfish's head. "I'm all right, Spike," she said. "Thanks to Max."

Rivet barked. "Niobe danger, Max!" he said.

# CHAPTER THREE

# BUGS

*What now?* thought Max as he kicked towards the surface, and his head broke the waves. Lia appeared at his side a moment later, putting on her Amphibio mask. Max looked past the reef towards the island a short swim away. There was his mother on the sandy beach, with more crab-like robots swarming around her, glinting in the sunshine, rearing up on their back legs and each clutching rusty hyperblades. They pressed closer and closer.

"INTRUDER! INTRUDER!" they cried.

"Riv, stay here and guard the sub," said Max.

His dogbot dipped beneath the water, and came up again clutching Max's blaster. "Thanks, boy," said Max, taking it from Rivet's metal jaws. "I hope I don't have to use it."

Together, he and Lia swam towards the shore. As they got closer, Max heard his mother trying to reason with the robots.

"Orion! Cassiopeia! It's me – Niobe! Don't you recognise me?"

"INTRUDER! INTRUDER!"

Max swam as fast as he could and waded out of the shallows.

"I made you!" yelled his mother. "I'm your leader!"

The robots' lights blinked. "TAKE TO LEADER!" said the one called Orion. He jabbed his hyperblade closer to Niobe, forcing her to skip to one side. Max levelled the blaster.

"Don't!" said his mother. "They're quite

harmless really, but if you shoot one, we'll be in real trouble."

Max tucked the blaster in his belt. *But if it gets nasty*, he thought, *I won't have any choice.*

"TAKE INTRUDER TO LEADER!"

Niobe sighed and rolled her eyes. "OK, OK! Let's go and find your leader." She shrugged hopelessly at Max and Lia. "They've all got some sort of bug," she said. "I have no choice."

"*Technology...*" said Lia.

Orion poked with his hyperblade again, and Niobe hurried up the beach, surrounding by the whirring robots. Max and Lia followed. "So much for a quick trip out!" murmured Max. "The sooner we fix this glitch, the better."

As they rose to the crest of a dune, Max saw that the island was bare apart from a few palm trees. It would only take a minute to walk right to the other side. So where was the lab?

While the other robots kept a tight circle

of hyperblades locked on Max's mum, Orion started beeping at a tree.

"It's gone completely mad…" said Lia.

A metal spike extended from the robot's body and slid into a tiny hole in the trunk. With a whirring sound, the sand at the base of the tree shifted and the whole trunk began to move sideways. Max gasped as he saw a dark hole appear in the ground below.

"A passage!" he said.

"Welcome to my old home," said Max's mum. "I just wish we were here under better circumstances."

The robots escorted them all down a steep metal ramp. As they descended into the cool air, glowing white lamps lit up along the walls. At the end a metal double door swished open.

Max couldn't believe his eyes.

Beyond was a state-of-the-art control room. There wasn't a single speck of sand on any of the gleaming panels. The banks of monitors were all operational, showing external views of the island, including Riv and Spike waiting in the shallows. More doors led off the main room, deeper into the underground complex.

"You built this?" said Max, eyes goggling.

"Well, I built the robots," said Max's mum, "and the robots built most of the facility. Impressive, huh?"

Max was speechless. Even Lia's eyes were wide with astonishment. The robots kept their hyperblades trained on Max's mother, but turned towards a wall-mounted box.

"LEADER. INTRUDER CAPTURED!" said Orion.

Light sprang from a tiny hole in the box, and a flickering hologram appeared – a life-size image of Max's mum in a red aquasuit.

"Welcome to the facility of Niobe North," said the hologram in Max's mum's voice. "If

this message is activated, I am in danger."

"Stop playback," said Max's mother. The hologram paused, obeying her voice-command. Niobe sighed. "I think I see the problem," she said. "They think *that*—" she pointed to the hologram – "is their leader!"

Lia snorted. Even Max couldn't help smiling.

"I'm your real leader," Niobe told the robots.

Orion cocked his head back and forth between the hologram and Max's mother.

"LEADER WEAR RED," he said.

Max's mother looked down at her purple aquasuit and sighed. "I only had one suit on the island," she said. "I guess they've never seen me in anything else."

Max jabbed Lia in the ribs. "Don't say *anything*," he said.

Lia stifled a laugh and gave her most innocent look. "So how are we going to sort this out?" she asked.

# CHAPTER FOUR

# CORA'S RETURN

"It's simple!" said Max. "We just need to override the island's security protocols."

Lia frowned, obviously confused.

"I mean we need to do some rewiring so that the robots don't see us as a threat," Max said.

Max's mother pointed to a wall panel at the far side of the room. "The master switches are behind there," she said.

As Max began to walk over, a few of the robots blocked his way with their hyperblades. "They're not stupid, are they?" he said. "We need a distraction. But what?"

"Leave it to me," said Lia. She darted across the room and snatched the hologram projector from the wall. The red-suited Niobe blinked off.

"LEADER! GIVE BACK LEADER!" cried the robots. They all turned on Lia, as she jumped up out of reach onto a table. The

robots circled her, waving their hyperblades. "GIVE BACK LEADER!"

Max ran to the wall panel and wrenched it open.

"Er…can you hurry?" said Lia. The robots were climbing on top of one another, forming a column to climb the table she was standing on. Max scanned the computer code.

"GIVE BACK LEADER!" squawked the robots.

Max trawled through the lines of code and located the bug. With a few taps on the touchscreen, he deleted it.

The robots lowered their blades as one and their eyes flashed green. They turned to Max's mother. "LEADER IS BACK! WELCOME LEADER!"

Lia jumped down from the table. "You took your time!" she said.

Niobe was patting each of the chirruping

robots on the head. "Thank you, Orion," she said. "And you, Perseus. Butes, you're looking a little stiff. We'll give you a drink of oil soon."

"I think your mum might be a little bit mad too," whispered Lia.

Niobe laughed. "I heard that! You try living on an island with no one to talk to," she said. "Trust me, any friends will do."

She went to another door, followed by the robots, and typed a code into the keypad. The door opened vertically with a soft swish.

"Do you want to see the lab?" she asked, stepping inside.

Max ran after her, and skidded to a halt at the door. "Whoa!" he said.

He found himself staring at a huge workshop, with stainless steel benches, more computers and a vast array of tech. "You were busy!" he said.

His mum's face fell. "I only wish I could have returned to Aquora sooner," she said. "But I wanted to straighten things out with your uncle first. I was so ashamed of him... and I still am."

Max hated to see his mum looking so sad. "Tell us about your inventions," he said. "They look amazing!"

Several half-finished contraptions hung from ceiling harnesses. One looked like an octopus with several tentacles, each ending in a different sort of grabber or suction tool.

"I called that one Octocleanse," said his mother. "It's designed to keep the ocean bed clear of human rubbish."

Max cast a sideways glance at Lia and saw her nodding with approval.

Another of the robots looked like a sphere with hundreds of small metal mouths. "And this?" Max asked.

His mother pressed a button and the sphere rolled across the floor, changing shape as it moved over the uneven surfaces. "It's called the Coralator," she said. "Those little mouths can repair coral reefs. It can fit into all sorts of awkward spaces."

Max marvelled at the design. His mother and his uncle were equally gifted, he realised.

*It's just that my uncle uses his skills for evil.*

"And what does this do?" asked Lia, who was looking at a helmet. There were sensors on the inside. Attached to the front was what looked like a speaker.

"That one I hadn't quite finished," said Niobe. "It's supposed to translate the wearer's thoughts into whale-speak."

Lia's eyes widened. "You're trying to mimic a Merryn's Aqua Powers!" she said.

Niobe nodded. "Not all tech is used for harm, you know," she said.

There was a screen positioned at the end of the room, and Max pressed the switch at the side. An electronic blueprint sprang up, showing a plan of a one-man sub with a drill at the front.

"That's called the Mole," said his mother. "It was only at design stage. See the retractable scoopers on either side? I'm rather pleased with them…"

She swiped her fingers across the screen and the design rotated. As she did so, Max caught a glimpse of the green brooch pinned high on her chest. It had been a gift from Roger the pirate, just before he disappeared.

"Mum," he said, pointing, "you never did explain why Roger gave you that."

His mother looked up, only briefly, then concentrated on the screen. "Who knows?" she said with a smile. "Maybe he's got a soft spot for me? Now, we should take the tech back to the *Dolphin* and head home. Callum will be wondering where we are."

They picked up the inventions between them and carried them back up the ramp and across the dunes. Rivet barked happily to see them again, and Spike leaped out of the water in excitement.

With the inventions finally stowed safely in the *Dolphin*'s hold, Niobe bade farewell to her trusty bots and climbed aboard. Orion and the others watched her, and Max couldn't help thinking they looked unhappy. As he steered the sub away from the island, Lia and Spike swam ahead, guiding them through the reef, followed by Rivet.

"Well, that was eventful," said Max, settling into his seat. "At least it was only Orion and his crew trying to kill us, rather than one of the Professor's creations."

*Back to Aquora*, he thought. *It's such a relief to have a break from battling the Professor's monsters!*

But out of nowhere, a screeching sound burrowed deep into his brain, and Max clamped his hands to his ears. Still he could hear it, like a saw biting into metal. *Where's it coming from? How is it getting through the sub's hull?*

Suddenly it stopped.

"What was that?" he said, as the ache in his head faded.

"I don't—" his mother began.

The sound came again, even louder, and Max fell forward from his chair, landing on his knees. He managed to open his eyes and saw his mother lying on the floor, her head in her hands and her mouth twisted in a grimace.

The noise stopped again and Max struggled to his feet.

"That horrible sound!" said Lia's voice, over the communicator. "Is it your lump of metal?"

His mother shook her head cautiously. "It's not the sub. I think it came from outside."

The screech returned. This time Max gripped the control panel and stared out, even though the terrible sound made his legs buckle. He couldn't see Lia or Spike, but

Rivet was hovering in the water ahead.

The scanners picked up a huge dark shape approaching from the starboard side. With a trembling hand, Max brought the *Dolphin* around. He saw at once what was making the sound, and his heart seemed to stop.

It was a creature – some kind of giant orca, or killer whale, its black and white bulk cutting through the water towards them. To Max's horror, he saw the creature had twin hyperblades lining its dorsal fin and tail. And when its mouth opened, he saw the glint of metal inside its throat.

"Uh-oh," said Lia's voice.

"There must be some kind of amplifying tech on its voice box," said Max. "That's why the screech is so bad."

The orca stopped ahead of them, making no move to attack. "I think we know who's behind this," said Niobe.

Max swallowed hard. "The Professor," he said. "It has to be. But how? He's in prison."

Then a familiar shape emerged from behind the Robobeast. Max sucked in a sharp breath. "It's my aquabike! The one that was stolen from the docks!"

"Greetings!" said a voice through the speakers. "Remember me?"

The voice belonged to Cora Blackheart.

# CHAPTER FIVE

# NO ESCAPE

Cora sat on the saddle of the aquabike, wearing a black wetsuit and breathing mask and leaning over the handlebars. The only recognisable feature was her long hair, flowing loose in the water.

"Hello again, Max!" she said. "Rekkar and I have been waiting for you to put in an appearance!"

Rivet suddenly shot towards her, gnashing his metal jaws. "Bad pirate!" he barked. Cora unholstered a blaster and fired. The shot sent

Riv spinning through the water, but Max
was relieved to see him turn tail and head
back towards the sub. As Cora put the pistol
away, Max noticed that she'd made some
adjustments to the bike since stealing it. Twin
rocket launchers bristled from the bike's sides.

The sight sent a chill down his spine.

"How did you make another Robobeast?" he asked over the communicator, trying to sound tough.

Cora laughed. "I didn't," she said. "Your uncle did, before he went and got himself caught. We had them stored on the *Pride of Blackheart*."

*Uh-oh*, thought Max. The night after the Aquoran forces had commandeered the pirate ship, an explosion had ripped a hole in its hull. *It must have been Cora, unleashing the Robobeasts. And now they're free to threaten Aquora again!*

."You might have foiled my plans to get the Kraken's Eye," snarled Cora, "but my revenge is going to be sweet!"

A rocket blasted from the bike.

"Look out, Max!" yelled Lia.

Max grabbed the steering column of the

*Dolphin* and yanked it sideways. The sub rolled and the rocket fizzed past, out into open water. But Max found himself staring right into the angry yellow eyes of Rekkar! With a thump, the orca's tail slammed into the side of the sub, and the shockwave hurled

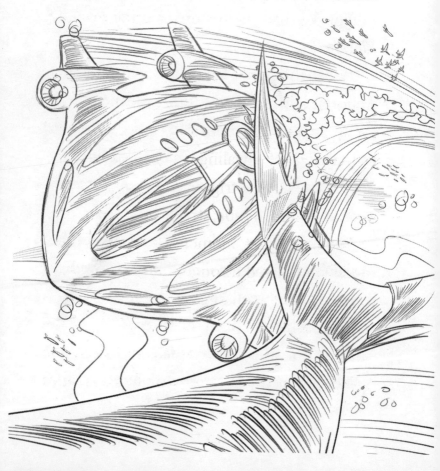

Max and his mother to the floor.

"This will be fun!" screeched Cora. "A dolphin's no match for a killer whale!"

Max found his feet and grabbed the controls, steering the sub out of harm's way.

"There's nowhere to run!" said Cora.

*I'm not running*, thought Max with a thin smile. *I'm just getting a clear shot.*

He turned the sub full circle, and his mother flicked several switches to turn on the weapons systems. "Let's show Cora what kind of dolphin she's dealing with," she said.

She pressed the trigger and a torpedo shot from the launch tube, straight towards Cora.

But at the last moment, a flash of black and white surged through the water. Rekkar's nose butted the missile off target in a stream of bubbles.

Max grabbed the controls and fired the sub's blasters right at the orca's flank. A series of direct hits exploded across Rekkar's side, driving it back. But as the water cleared, he saw they'd had no effect whatsoever. Out of the corner of his eye, Max saw Lia darting towards Cora on Spike, looking determined. The Merryn princess had no weapon other than her pet's serrated sword.

Cora gunned the aquabike out of range. Lia gave chase, and the two zipped through the water, evenly matched for speed and agility. But Max knew that Spike would tire first. Cora was distracted, but it couldn't last.

Rekkar had recovered, and let out another shriek. The sound seemed to make Max's bones ache, and he fell to the ground. By the time he managed to stand, Rekkar was nowhere to be seen. Lia was still chasing Cora, neither one of them apparently affected by the terrible sound. *Rekkar must be able to target its soundwaves*, Max thought.

"Where's it gone?" said Niobe.

Max pointed in horror to the radar, where a huge shape was approaching from the rear of the *Dolphin*.

"It's behind…"

*SLAM!*

The force of the impact sent the sub spinning through the water towards the seabed. Max was thrown across the cabin, then bashed against the walls. He found himself lying on the ceiling. The *Dolphin* was stranded on her roof on the bottom of the ocean with alarm lights flashing and sirens blaring. *Where's Lia?* he thought dimly.

His mother helped him upright, and he noticed with a shock that she was bleeding from a cut on her head.

Cora's voice filled the sub. "You didn't really think I'd finished with you, did you? Cora never forgets who her enemies are!"

Through the upside-down bubble screen, Cora appeared on the bike, close enough to touch the plexiglass. Now Max could see her at close range, he realised her helmet wasn't just a breathing apparatus. Over one eye was a transparent visor, with wiring to some sort of headset.

*She must use it to control Rekkar*, he thought. *If I could take that off her, we'd have one less problem to worry about.*

"This was a little bit too easy," said Cora, "but it's time we said our farewells. Of course, yours will be a permanent goodbye."

She opened the seat compartment on the bike and pulled out a fist-sized object. Max's heart sank. *A marine grenade.*

Cora pulled the pin, and tossed the grenade on top of the sub. Max heard it bounce a couple of times then come to rest. Cora gave a little wave, backing the bike away.

Max scrambled to the controls, but nothing worked. They'd all gone dead.

"Get down!" he shouted, scrambling behind one of the seats.

*BOOM!*

The force of the blast hit Max like a wave. He was aware of water rushing into the sub. He saw his mother tossed like a rag doll to the back of the cabin as the *Dolphin* rolled over. When the bubbles cleared, he saw that the top hatch had been blown open, obliterated by the grenade. Pieces of debris littered the ocean floor and the sub was completely filled with water. He glanced around and saw his mother outside on the seabed. She must have been thrown clear. She lay face down, partly hidden beneath a section of the torn hull. And she wasn't moving.

"No!" Max cried. He swam out of the broken vessel to her side. "Mum?" he said.

Rivet joined him, and Max saw a blackened scar on his snout where Cora's blaster had hit.

With a swish of bubbles, Lia appeared at his side on Spike. Above them the ominous shadow of Rekkar circled in the water, with Cora riding the bike above the remains of the sub. He didn't think she'd spotted him, because her blasters were still pointed at the remains of the *Leaping Dolphin*.

Max cradled his mother's body, then pulled her collar aside, feeling for a pulse at her throat. To his relief, he found a soft heartbeat. Her gills were working too, but only weakly. The green brooch shone brightly in the water.

"Lia, use your Aqua Powers to summon help," he said urgently. "Try to keep Cora and Rekkar at bay."

Lia pressed her temples and her brow furrowed. A moment later her eyes flicked open, full of despair. "It's still not working,"

she said. "I don't know why!"

The *Dolphin* rocked as Cora fired her blasters at the wrecked shell, cackling madly. The hull was tough, but if she kept up the attack, there wouldn't be much left.

"We have to get my mum to the surface," said Max.

Rekkar's screech shook the water, and Max

struggled to hold onto his mother. The sound wasn't as bad as before, so Max guessed the orca wasn't directing it right at them. Looking up, he saw the Robobeast circling. It wouldn't be long before it discovered them.

His mother stirred, and straight away her eyes seemed to focus on something beyond. "What's that?" she mumbled.

Max followed her gaze and for a moment he forgot about the giant killer whale above. Beyond the wreck of the *Leaping Dolphin*, he saw a strange patch of shimmering water. It looked like a heat haze, but underwater. Cora must have spied it too, because she edged the aquabike away. Rekkar followed, as if even the Robobeast was wary.

Max had no idea what the shimmering water was, but he didn't have time to figure it out. "This might be our only chance to get away," he said. "Come on!"

He kicked upwards, dragging his mother with him. The patch of shimmering water seemed to follow them.

"Quicker!" said Lia.

Max glanced back and saw the water begin to spin like an underwater tornado. He swam harder, clawing through the water with his free hand. The *Leaping Dolphin* was swallowed by the surging current.

"Riv, get us out of here!" yelled Max. The dogbot swam ahead, and Max reached for his collar. All the time, the pull from below grew stronger.

Then Lia and Spike were gone, snatched by the current. His mother was torn from his grasp. Max opened his mouth to scream, but didn't get the chance. The whirlpool grabbed him firmly, and in a blinding flash of light, it yanked him down.

Everything went dark.

# CHAPTER SIX

# THE LOST LAGOON

Max felt the seabed under his back. He was lying down, and his whole body ached.

*I must have blacked out...*

But something wasn't right. He was breathing air into his lungs, not water. *Which means...*

He opened his eyes and saw the sky. He heard birds calling in the distance.

"I'm on land," he croaked.

He moved his hands, and even that sent a wave of pain through his arms. His fingertips moved in soft white sand. *Where am I?*

Memories of the battle with Cora and Rekkar flooded into his mind, and panic rose in his chest. *Mum? Lia?*

Max sat bolt upright, and immediately wished he hadn't. His head swam and he almost retched. He reached up and touched a tender spot on the side of his head. A lump was already growing.

Looking down, he saw his wetsuit was ripped and scuffed.

But he was alive.

"Stuck, Max! Broken!" barked a familiar but muffled voice.

Max stood up and looked around. He was on the shore of a large island, near the water's edge. Palm trees rustled in a light breeze. A few paces away, Rivet's back legs and tail propeller were sticking out of a sand dune. Max scrambled over and heaved his dogbot out. Rivet shook his head and a few grains of sand tipped out of his ear sensors. "Thanks, Max!" he barked.

"We've got to find Mum and Lia," said Max. "Let's split up."

"Rivet find!" said his dogbot, lowering his metal snout to the ground. Max followed the shoreline, shouting their names.

"Lia! Mum!"

"We're here!" Lia called back. Max looked out to sea and saw her in the shallows, with Spike bobbing at her side. There was no sign of his mother. He began to feel sick.

*What if I've lost her again?* he thought.

"I can't find my Amphibio mask," said Lia, then ducked back underwater to take a breath.

Max looked around and caught sight of it,

hanging by a strap from a palm tree branch.
"Hold on!" he said. It took a bit of scrambling,
but he managed to shin his way up the trunk
and pluck the mask free. He jumped down
and tossed it to the Merryn girl. Leaving
Spike, she waded ashore, strapping the mask
over her face.

"I thought I saw someone lying further
along the sand," she said. From her quiet
tone and frown, Max feared the worst.

Rivet barked. "Max mum! Come quick!"

Max and Lia ran round a dune and found Rivet crouched near Niobe. She was lying on her front, arms splayed.

Max skidded to his knees at her side. "Help me turn her over!" he said, his voice breaking.

Half her face was coated in hair and wet sand, but as soon as they put her on her back she stirred. Max's heart leaped with relief.

"Don't move too much," said Max. "You

might have broken bones."

"I'm fine," said his mum, sitting up slowly. Her eyes widened. "What is this place?"

Max shrugged and stared around, looking for clues. "I have no idea. We were underwater."

"Maybe we died in that whirlpool and this is the afterlife," said Lia.

Rivet started digging in the sand. "I'm pretty sure robotic dogs don't have an afterlife," said Max.

They all heard a fast chirruping from the water. Spike was waving his sword. Lia stood up and went closer.

"He says there's something strange in the water further out," she said.

Spike gave a few more clicks and squeaks.

"A shimmering barrier," Lia translated. "He can't pass through it."

Niobe drew a sharp breath. "Oh no!"

"What?" said Lia and Max at once.

"Have you ever heard of the Lost Lagoon?" asked Max's mother.

"Lost?" barked Rivet.

Max racked his brains. "Didn't Gran tell me stories about it when I was little? A legendary place. Not on any charts. Not even real!" He remembered the stories more clearly now. *Shipwrecks, sailors driven mad, terrible creatures living in the depths.*

"The thing about the Lost Lagoon…" he said, slowly, "…is that there's no way out."

"Lost!" said Rivet again, his tail hanging between his legs.

# CHAPTER SEVEN

# UNDERWATER EXPEDITION

Max thought about his dad, back on Aquora. He'd be looking for them by now, and probably starting to panic. And with more Robobeasts on the rampage, the sooner they got word to Aquora, the better for everyone.

"Maybe Dad will lead a rescue party," he said hopefully.

His mum shook her head regretfully. "The Lost Lagoon isn't like that," she said. "You can't find it. It finds *you*."

Max's heart sank. He'd only just reunited his family and now it was shattered again.

"Wait!" said Lia. "The Forgotten Shores!"

"Pardon?" said Max.

"That's what we Merryn call this place!" said Lia. "Not the Lost Lagoon. We have old tales too, you know."

"And?" said Niobe.

"And there *is* a way to escape," said Lia. "At least, there's a story about a way to escape. I remember my father telling me. See, there was this explorer who got stuck on the Forgotten Shores. But he got out by making a special compass. It showed him how to escape. If we could build the same compass…"

"How did he make it?" asked Max.

Lia screwed up her brow in thought. "Let me see… There's a song about it. The compass was made from four metals, but I only know the

Merryn names: Galdium, Rullium, Fennum and, let me see…" She stuck her tongue in her cheek as she thought. "Barrum!" she said at last.

Niobe shook her head. "I know of those metals," she said. "But they're all very rare. The only one I'd even know where to start looking for is Galdium. It comes from certain underwater volcanoes."

"We could use the *Leaping Dolphin*'s scanners," said Max. Then his hope sagged. "If we knew where she was, that is."

"We do!" said Lia. "She's on the seabed, not far from here. Spike spotted her earlier."

"Great!" said Max's mum. She tried to stand, but sank back with a grimace, clutching her side. Max was afraid she'd cracked a rib in the fight with Cora.

"Wait here," he said. "We'll go."

Leaving his mum on the beach to recover,

Max and the others dived below the water. Max glanced about nervously as they swam. Who knew what lived in the Lost Lagoon? Soon he spied the *Leaping Dolphin*, buried in the sand on the seabed. Several alarms flashed within, lighting up the water with a red glow. The front screen was intact, but the top section of the sub's hull was a mess of charred, torn metal. Max swam aboard the water-filled vessel. Thankfully the *Dolphin* was built to withstand flooding – the circuitry was all watertight. He disabled the flashing alarms and assessed the damage. One thruster had gone completely and another registered half power. The scanners, heat-seeker and radar were all down.

Max climbed into the pilot's seat and turned on the engine. It started with a grinding sound, but then settled to a hum. He gripped the controls and activated the base thrusters.

Slowly, the sub lifted from the seabed.

Lia gave a whoop from outside, and Max smiled. In fits and starts, he guided the *Dolphin* back towards the island. Filled with water, the vessel was hard to manoeuvre, and the steering column juddered as he fought to control it. Finally, he beached the sub on the sand, a metal carcass dredged from the deep. Max hit the drainage switch and water began to pour

out from the bottom of the sub, soaking the sand all around it.

"My poor ship!" said his mother, surveying the damage as she clambered into the dripping interior. "Is the toposcan working?"

Max tried to activate the scanner which mapped the seabed, but it remained blank.

"Sorry, Mum," he said.

Niobe's shoulders sank. "That's going to make things tricky. Finding an underwater volcano without scanners is like finding a needle in a haystack."

"Rivet find!" said the dogbot, jumping up and down beside them.

"Of course!" said Max. "I adapted the topography scanning tech for Riv. He's not got the same range, but it might be enough."

He twisted a dial behind one of Rivet's ears. A 3D map sprang up from a tiny projector.

"You're a genius!" said Niobe.

"Don't encourage him," muttered Lia.

"Scan the area, Riv," said Max.

The map shifted, showing the landscape of the seabed all around, with dips and rises, trenches and ridges. "There!" said Max, pointing to a conical mountain quite a way from the island. From the crater shape at its peak, it had to be a volcano. "Riv, transfer coordinates to the *Dolphin*'s computers."

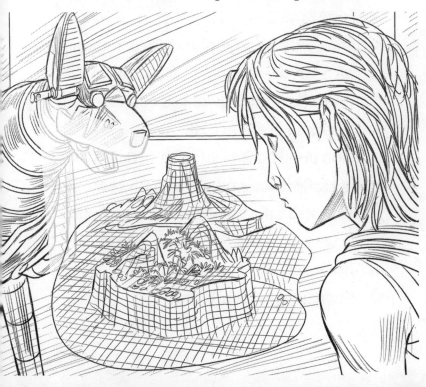

Rivet touched one paw to a socket on the control panel. His eyes flashed as the data was transmitted.

"Now we just have to get the *Dolphin* shipshape," said Niobe. "Anyone see a shipyard around here?"

Max laughed. "It's a bit crude, but we could use palm bark to block the hole." He went to the back of the vessel and found the toolkit. "Let's get to it."

It took over an hour of backbreaking work to patch up the *Leaping Dolphin*, and when they'd finished she still looked battle-scarred and rather sorry for herself.

Niobe stood back, one eyebrow raised. "We won't know if she's fully watertight until we get her back in the water, but it'll have to do."

"I'll see you out there," said Lia. She took off her mask and ran out into the water, where she climbed onto Spike's back.

Sitting at the controls again, Max eased the sub back into the water. He sent her into a dive, checking the bark patch as they dipped beneath the waves. "It looks sound," he said.

Engaging the engines, Max set the wounded *Dolphin* on a course towards the location of the volcano. With her left thrusters damaged, he had to steer constantly to keep her straight. But soon he spied the volcano in the distance. It rose like a giant mountain from the seabed, dark and looming. Ash was being belched from the crater, turning the water black.

"Uh-oh," said his mother. "We don't have long. That ash means it's in the early stages of eruption."

"What does Galdium even look like?" asked Lia, from outside. At least the communication systems were still working.

"It's bright blue," said Niobe. "It's found right in the crater."

Max swallowed. "How did I know you were going to say that? Take us closer."

Niobe nudged the steering column and the *Leaping Dolphin* drifted towards the volcano's spewing crater. *If this goes wrong, there'll be nothing left of any of us*, thought Max.

The volcano was starting to fall apart. Its slopes shifted, then broke. Panicking, Max hit the reverse thrusters. "It's going to blow!"

"No!" said Lia. "That isn't the volcano – it's rock turtles!"

Max paused the vessel, peering closer. After a moment he could see what Lia was talking about. It wasn't the volcano that was disintegrating. Huge black-shelled creatures had been clinging to the slopes, and now they were swimming towards the *Leaping Dolphin*.

"Don't worry!" called Lia. "They're peaceful creatures."

She'd barely finished speaking when the first of the turtles, beady eyes staring straight ahead, smashed into the *Dolphin*'s watershield. A crack spread across the plexiglass.

"Are you sure?" said Niobe. A second turtle rammed them, making the sub shudder. "They don't seem very peaceful to me!"

# CHAPTER EIGHT

# INTO THE FIRE

Another two turtles hit the screen heavily, and the cracks spread. "We'll flood again if they break through," said Max.

"I don't understand," said Lia. "We keep rock turtles as pets at home. They're gentle!"

"Maybe the Lost Lagoon has changed them," said Max. As more turtles swam towards them, he pressed the sub's blaster trigger. "I hope this still works."

It didn't. The blaster gave out nothing but a feeble flash of light.

"Oh dear," said Niobe.

But to Max's surprise, the army of turtles left the viewing screen alone and all swam towards the blaster barrels.

"Maybe it reminds them of the volcano's lava," said Lia. "Do it again."

Max did as she said, filling the water with another flash of light. The turtles swam in a circle around the blaster cannon.

"Try to keep them busy with the blaster, Mum," said Max.

"Where are you going?" asked Niobe.

Max took a deep breath. "Into the volcano crater," he said. "To get the Galdium."

Max's mother shook her head. "You can't! It's too dangerous. It might blow any minute."

"Exactly," said Max. "And if it erupts, we might never get the Galdium. If we can't make the compass, we'll never get home." He went to the hatch.

"Wait!" said Niobe. "Go to the equipment store and get a heatproof flask. Liquid Galdium is incredibly hot."

Max went to the cupboard and found a sturdy thermo-flask.

"Good luck, son," said his mother.

"Careful, Max!" barked Rivet.

Max nodded and made his way through the airlock. Out in the water, Lia was waiting on Spike, keeping an eye on the turtles.

"I'll cover you," she said. "Try not to get

yourself killed, Max."

Max smiled as best he could and kicked towards the crater. He took one glance back at the turtles, hovering near the flaming blaster like drones, before swimming on. He could feel the currents of heat all around him. The water seemed to tremble as the volcano shook. At last he reached its rocky mouth, and peering over the lip of the crater, he saw the orange glow of lava deep within.

*Here goes nothing*, he thought, and dived into the abyss.

Inside, the water felt like a hot bath, and the ash made it hard to see. The vibrations were even worse, buffeting his body from side to side. Max caught a glimpse of a fluorescent blue streak in the bubbling lava below.

*Galdium!*

The water was growing hotter and hotter, almost unbearable. How long before it became too much? He reached the lava level and saw more pools of Galdium, like blue oil spills. Holding the flask's handle, he reached as close as he dared. The heat on his hand was agony, but he gritted his teeth and scooped the blue liquid metal into the thermo-flask.

Max jerked back as a fiery tongue of lava licked upwards. More bubbles sprang up on the lava's surface, popping and spraying molten rock dangerously close to his face. The volcano rumbled, and the lava began to move towards him.

*Oh no!* Max thought. *It's erupting!*

The Galdium had turned solid in the flask already. Max sped upwards, away from the rising tide of molten rock. The entire mountain shook, blurring his vision as he swam. He thought about nothing but getting out, and swam harder than ever before. Fear gave him strength as a wave of superheated water pressed him from beneath.

Max burst from the crater, driven upwards and away by a surge of dirty water. He rolled over and over in the water, but kept a firm grip on the flask. He caught a glimpse of lava pouring over the lip of the volcano and spreading out into the water like a wave. Where was Lia? Was she safe? He saw turtles

swimming away in panic as the blast-force sent him spinning towards the *Leaping Dolphin*.

Terror gripped him. *Mum! She's in there…*

"Get out!" he screamed. "Get out!"

But the roar of the volcano drowned his cries. The seabed rushed towards him. He held out his hands, but it was too late.

*Smack!*

He must have lost consciousness, because he woke up floating near a boulder. Dust particles filled the water and the volcano had stopped spewing molten rock. He cast a desperate glance towards the sub.

*No…*

It was coated in a layer of still-glowing lava, slowly eating away at the hull like some terrible acid. Max dropped the flask.

"Mum!" he cried. He swam towards the sub, and with each stroke his hopes faded. Nothing could survive that – the water inside would be way past boiling point. Max's heart sank. "Mum," he said again, weakly.

*I just got her back...*

Someone touched his shoulder.

"It's OK, honey. I'm safe."

Max could barely look, but when he did, he saw his mother swimming beside him, a smile on her face. Behind her Lia floated on Spike, with Rivet beside them.

"Lava eat sub!" barked Rivet.

Max hugged his mum. "I thought you were..."

"Well, I'm not," she said. "When the eruption started, I got out of there double-quick." She nodded towards the *Leaping Dolphin*. "It's a shame, though. All that hard work. I hope she's salvageable."

Max glanced at the seabed, and saw the flask he'd dropped. He swam down and fetched it. "I got the Galdium!" he said. "Now we have the first part of the—"

A terrible screech filled the water, turning his bones to jelly.

"Oh no!" said Lia, staring beyond him. "It can't be…we haven't seen it since we got to the Lost Lagoon!"

Max turned and saw a black and white monster in the distance, heading steadily towards them. He couldn't believe his eyes. *Surely the Robobeast can't be here too!*

But as the huge shape moved closer, there could be no doubt. Rekkar had followed them – and now they were trapped together.

# CHAPTER NINE

# REKKAR'S REVENGE

"It must have got caught in that shimmering water too," said Niobe.

*I wonder if that means Cora's close behind,* thought Max. But right now, there were bigger things to worry about.

Hanging in the water, with just his hyperblade, he felt hopelessly outmatched. If only they had the *Leaping Dolphin* for protection. Niobe drew her blaster pistol.

"We've got no chance," said Max, "unless…"

He looked at Lia, who was gripping Spike's neck. "Can you talk to it with your Aqua Powers?" he asked.

"I told you," said Lia. "They aren't working!"

"Try again," said Max. "It's our only chance."

Lia closed her eyes, and Max saw her jaw tense. Rekkar nosed ever closer, and the hyperblades flashed along its fins and tail.

Lia sighed and opened her eyes. "Nothing," she said. "I don't understand! Something's interfering – it was the same when we left Aquora."

The orca put on a sudden burst of speed, its monstrous form shooting through the water, then turning with a mighty flick of its tail. They all dodged as the powerful fins swished past, catching them in a wave. Rekkar opened its mouth and screeched again. This close, the sound seemed to split Max's head in two

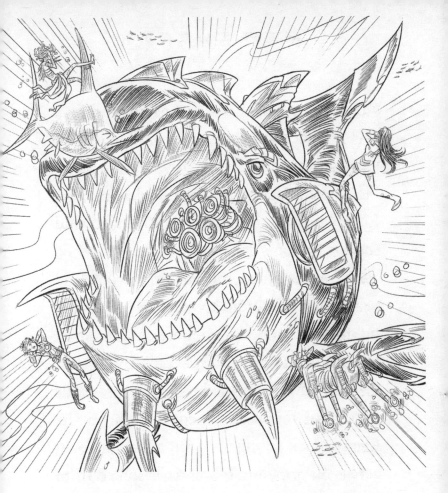

– he felt like his brain was melting! Holding
his hands to his ears eased the pain a little,
but when he drew them away, he saw blood
on his palms. Rekkar was literally making his
ears bleed. Spike thrashed in the water, and
Lia tumbled off his back.

The killer whale slid past again, and Max saw a bladed fin slashing towards him. He snatched his hyperblade out just in time to block the attack, but as the blades met, the force knocked him back. He lunged and scarred Rekkar's flank, and the orca screeched again. Max folded himself into a ball and prayed for the sound to end. How could he fight this Robobeast when he couldn't even take his hands away from his ears? He looked up and saw a fin-blade spinning towards him once more. He tried to roll, but he wasn't quick enough. He felt a stinging pain across his arm, and blood trails spilled from a slash in his wetsuit. Rekkar turned on him, opening his jaws wide. Max saw hundreds of razor-sharp teeth, ready to tear him apart.

*ZZZAP!*

Smoke exploded from Rekkar's forehead, and all at once the killer whale backed off.

Max turned and saw his mother holding the blaster pistol in both hands. "Get away from my son!" she shouted.

Rekkar blew a mouthful of bubbles and writhed in pain. But Max saw the scorch mark on its skin wasn't serious. *A hundred blasters might do the trick, but one is just a nuisance to a Robobeast this size.*

"Thank you!" he gasped.

"I don't have much charge," said Niobe, nodding to the gun, but keeping it trained on the orca. "Let's hope it doesn't call my bluff."

"If we can get back to the *Dolphin* and fix her blasters, they might be enough," said Max.

Even as he said the words, he realised it was a long shot.

"Good thinking," said Niobe, "but we need a distraction."

As if on cue, Rivet shot out from beneath the Robobeast and clamped his metal jaws around the orca's fin. Max saw the teeth sink into its flesh.

Rekkar thrashed, but Rivet held on stubbornly. *He'll get himself shaken to nuts and bolts in no time!*

"Let's go, quickly!" said Max.

He and his mother swam side by side towards the *Leaping Dolphin*.

As they neared the submarine's lava-crusted hull, Lia shot up from the seabed on Spike. In her hands she trailed lengths of fronded green seaweed. "This is blotweed," she said. "My father uses it to help him sleep at night – it muffles sound."

"Like ear plugs!" said Max, taking a handful of blotweed and stuffing it in his ears. Niobe did the same.

But it wasn't enough to block Rivet's

panicked howl as Rekkar shook him free. With a bat of his tail, the killer whale sent Max's dogbot spinning away like a giant ball bearing.

Then the Robobeast swam towards them at speed. Max, Lia and Niobe dived behind the *Dolphin*, and the sub shuddered as Rekkar's nose thumped into it. Close up,

Max realised the damage to the *Dolphin* wasn't as bad as he'd first thought. The lava had only eaten part of the hull away. In fact, now it was hardened, the sub was probably more watertight than before. Rekkar raked his tail across the sub's hull with an angry screech. The blotweed in Max's ears muffled the sound a little, but it was still impossible to move until it stopped.

"We need to draw it away," shouted Niobe. "Otherwise it'll completely destroy the sub."

"That doesn't sound like much of a plan," said Lia. "Out in the open, we're like sardines to the slaughter."

"And if the *Leaping Dolphin* is too badly damaged, we're stuck here in the Lost Lagoon for ever," said Max, "leaving Cora and her Robobeast on the loose. I say we take our chances. If we can get back to the island, we might be safe."

Lia frowned. She looked seriously unconvinced.

The sub suddenly shot away, swept aside by Rekkar's tail. Nothing stood between them and the Robobeast but empty water.

"So much for getting away," said Max.

The killer whale eyed them, and its wide mouth seemed to grin. Max tasted its foul fishy breath in the water, and terror made his stomach turn to liquid.

Rekkar surged towards them.

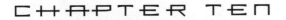

# CHAPTER TEN

## FREEING REKKAR

The teeth were less than an arm's length away when Rekkar stopped dead in the water. Max realised he could hear another screech, and it wasn't coming from the Robobeast.

He turned and saw Lia, her mouth wide open.

"Is that you?" he asked, gobsmacked.

She nodded, her face straining as she changed pitch. Rekkar rolled slightly, cocking

its head curiously. It screeched back, quieter
than before, but still enough to make Max
wince. Lia responded with the same note,
and the angry haze seemed to disappear
from the orca's eyes.

"That's incredible!" said Niobe.

Lia blushed. "I can't use my Aqua Powers,
but I thought I'd try what I know of her own

language," she said. "Rekkar's a girl, by the way."

The killer whale rolled over in the water, letting out a series of cheeps.

"She's just lonely, I think," said Lia. "Killer whales are very social animals. They normally swim in pods. Whatever tech the Professor has used is making her act against her natural instincts."

"My brother must have trapped this one and kept her captive before he added the tech," said Niobe. "Poor thing!"

"Whatever you're saying, keep saying it," said Max. "I'll see if I can free her from the robotics."

As he edged closer, Rekkar suddenly snapped her jaws at him. Max jerked back to avoid being chomped in two.

Lia let out a series of reassuring chirps. "She's scared," said the Merryn girl. "She doesn't know who to trust."

"Er…here, fishy-fishy," Max soothed.

Lia sighed. "An orca is a mammal, not a fish." She gave a few more chirrups. "Try again."

Max swallowed and pointed to the killer whale's fin. "I just want to help you," he said. As he swam closer, his heart thumped in his chest. Every instinct yelled at him to run away, but he forced himself nearer. Rekkar's beady eye watched him intently.

"Please tell her I'm a friend," said Max. "And that I taste awful!"

"This is no time for jokes," said Max's mum. "Be careful, son."

Lia sang to the orca in soft, lilting tones. "She's fighting the tech, but it's hard for her. It hurts."

As Max reached the Robobeast's flank, she lifted one of her side fins. He peered beneath and got a jolt of surprise. It wasn't the usual neat work he expected from his uncle. The tech was unfinished, with plates only loosely bolted and a few wires hanging free. Rekkar had a nasty sore where her fin joined her body, and Max guessed some of the robotics had already worked themselves loose.

"I don't think the Professor had finished with you," he said, stroking the orca's black fin. "Hold still and I'll see what I can do."

He used his hyperblade tip to cut away the remaining robotics carefully, then swam to the tail to do the same. He had to lean all his weight against the hilt to prise loose the tech. When it was done, his hyperblade was bent in the middle. "Oh, great!" he muttered.

Meanwhile Lia swam to the ocean floor and came back with more seaweed. She fed it to Spike, who chewed it to a mush, then spat it back into her hands.

Chirping quietly to keep Rekkar calm, Lia pressed the weed mulch into the orca's wound. "That should help the healing process," she said.

As the last of the robotics fell to the ocean floor, Rekkar shuddered with pleasure and chirruped happily. She pressed her nose towards Lia and Niobe, who stroked it.

"I don't need to speak whale to know she's grateful," said Max's mother.

Max and his companions watched in silence as the killer whale turned and drifted off into the depths. Another creature was free of the Professor's cruelty. Max just hoped she could find a peaceful life here in the Lost Lagoon.

"I guess we should get going," he said to the others. "There are three more metals to find if we're going to make the compass we need to get out of here."

He swam towards the *Leaping Dolphin*, expecting the worst. Most of the sub was scarred and scorched in places, and much of the roof was now made of solid rock where the lava had hardened to a shell.

Thankfully, the airlock was undamaged. Max and his mum climbed aboard with Rivet, leaving Lia and Spike outside.

Only the emergency lights were on. Max went to the control panel, and crossing his fingers, switched on the engines. He heard the satisfying hum of the thrusters on standby.

"She's working!" he said, relief flooding through his veins.

His mother jumped into the seat beside him, a smile on her face. "We may be stuck in the Lost Lagoon, but at least we've still got transport."

Max eased on the forward thrusters and the sub pushed through the water, away from the volcano. A few dark shapes slid past – rock turtles returning home.

The vid screen suddenly fizzed into life, and the sub's automated voice announced, "Incoming message alert."

Max pushed the receive button.

"I bet it's your father," said Niobe, with a hopeful smile. "He's going to be mad…"

But the face that popped up wasn't Callum's. Max's stomach clenched.

"Nice to see you again," Cora Blackheart said. But her narrow eyes looked anything but pleased.

In the background Max saw a blue sky and palm trees. A beach. And if he wasn't mistaken, it was the same stretch of sand they'd washed up on.

"She's in the Lost Lagoon!" he said.

"That's right," cackled Cora. "And guess what? I've brought a few friends..."

Niobe frowned. "You haven't got any friends, Cora."

The pirate put on a hurt face. "Now, now," she said. "No need to be mean. When I say 'friends', I do of course mean 'killer Robobeasts'. Three more, to be precise – the most advanced your devious brother created. And they'll be coming for you – very soon."

Max switched off the screen and looked around him. The *Leaping Dolphin* was a wreck, his hyperblade was bent in the middle and his mum's blaster was empty. Oh, and Lia didn't seem to have her Aqua Powers.

*Things could be worse*, he thought, *but I'm not quite sure how.*

"Max scared?" asked Rivet, rubbing his snout against Max's leg.

Max glanced at his loyal robodog, then

across at the look of determination on his mother's face. Lia swished across their path on Spike.

"Yes, I'm scared," admitted Max, "but this Quest is far from over. We'll find those metals for the compass so we can get out of here. And we'll stop Cora and her Robobeasts too, even if it kills us. Got it?"

"Got it," said Lia through the speakers.

Max's mother laid a hand across his shoulder. "Got it," she said.

Rivet let out a fierce bark.

*While we stick together*, thought Max, *we've got a chance.*

Don't miss Max's next Sea Quest
adventure, when he faces

TRAGG
THE ICE BEAR

# COLLECT ALL THE BOOKS IN SEA QUEST SERIES 4:

# THE LOST LAGOON

978 1 40832 861 3

978 1 40832 863 7

978 1 40832 865 1

978 1 40832 867 5

# OUT NOW!

Look out for all the books in
Sea Quest Series 5:

# THE CHAOS QUADRANT

SYTHID THE SPIDER CRAB

BRUX THE TUSKED TERROR

VENOR THE SEA SCORPION

MONOTH THE SPIKED DESTROYER

## OUT IN APRIL 2015!

Don't miss the
BRAND NEW
Special Bumper Edition:

# DRAKKOS
## THE OCEAN KING

978 1 40832 848 4

## OUT IN NOVEMBER 2014

# WIN AN EXCLUSIVE
# GOODY BAG

In every Sea Quest book the Sea Quest logo is
hidden in one of the pictures. Find the logos in books
13-16, make a note of which pages they appear on and
go online to enter the competition at

## www.seaquestbooks.co.uk

Each month we will put all of the correct entries into a draw
and select one winner to receive a special Sea Quest goody bag.

You can also send your entry on a postcard to:

Sea Quest Competition, Orchard Books,
338 Euston Road, London, NW1 3BH

Don't forget to include your name and address!

## GOOD LUCK

### Closing Date: Nov 30th 2014

# IF YOU LIKE SEA QUEST, YOU'LL LOVE BEAST QUEST!

**FREE COLLECTOR CARDS INSIDE!**

## Series 1: COLLECT THEM ALL!

An evil wizard has enchanted the magical beasts of Avantia. Only a true hero can free the beasts and save the land. Is Tom the hero Avantia has been waiting for?

978 1 84616 483 5

978 1 84616 482 8

978 1 84616 484 2

978 1 84616 486 6

978 1 84616 485 9

978 1 84616 487 3

# DON'T MISS THE
# BRAND NEW SERIES OF:

## Series 15: VELMAL'S REVENGE

978 1 40833 487 4

978 1 40833 489 8

978 1 40833 491 1

978 1 40833 493 5

# COMING SOON!